Megan

8

Aeppl The 28

Megan weir   8

APPrl the 28th

For Henry & Claudia

First published in Great Britain 1992 by
Julia MacRae
an imprint of The Random House Group
20 Vauxhall Bridge Road, London, SW1V 2SA

Random House Australia (Pty) Ltd
20 Alfred Street, Milsons Point, Sydney, NSW 2061

Random House New Zealand Ltd
PO Box 40-086, Glenfield, Auckland 10, New Zealand

Random House South Africa (Pty) Ltd
PO Box 337, Bergvlei, 2021, South Africa

Printed in Singapore

British Library Cataloguing in Publication Data
Newcome, Zita
Little lion
I. Title II. Newcome Robert
823.914 [J]

ISBN 1-85681-181-6

Little — LION

Robert & Zita Newcome

Julia MacRae Books

LONDON SYDNEY AUCKLAND JOHANNESBURG

There was once a little lion who lived in a place where the jungle met the desert.

He played all day with his brothers and sisters and when he was good his father would say:

"Well done, Little Lion. One day you will grow up to be King of the Jungle."

Now his father was very wise, so Little Lion listened
to these words and believed them to be true.

But before Little Lion was fully grown, a terrible thing happened. Hunters came and shot at his family, scattering them in all directions. Little Lion ran and ran and when at last he stopped, the other lions were nowhere to be seen. He was all alone.

For three days he searched for his family and, as time passed, he grew very hungry, very tired and very frightened. But he kept saying to himself, "I mustn't give up, I mustn't give up. One day I will be King of the Jungle."

At last, almost too tired to walk, he crept into a hole in the ground to hide. Suddenly a large snake appeared. "What are you doing, Little Lion," hissed the snake, "hiding in a hole like a tiny mouse? You look sssmall and ssstupid, not at all like the King of the Jungle."

Little Lion was frightened, but then a voice inside him said, "Keep going, Little Lion, keep going." So he jumped up and ran away from the slithery snake.

After a while he stopped to hide in the shadow of a rock. Suddenly a large hyena appeared. "What are you doing, Little Lion," barked the hyena, "hiding behind a rock like a tiny lizard? You look weak and weedy, not at all like the King of the Jungle."

Again Little Lion was frightened, but then a voice inside him said, "Keep going, Little Lion, keep going." So he jumped up and ran away from the horrid hyena.

After a while he stopped to hide in some tall reeds by a river. Suddenly a large crocodile appeared. "What are you doing, Little Lion," croaked the crocodile, "hiding in the reeds like a tiny rat? You look cowardly and creepy, not at all like the King of the Jungle."

And for the third time Little Lion was frightened,
but then a voice inside him said, "Keep going, Little Lion,
keep going." So he jumped up and ran away from the cruel
crocodile.

By now he was on the edge of the desert and he watched a herd of enormous elephants walk past. He felt very small. "Maybe it's true,"

he said to himself. "Maybe I am small and stupid, weak and weedy, cowardly and creepy. If so, how can I ever be King of the Jungle?"

But then he saw a wise old monkey sitting alone by a tree. "Please help me, Mr Monkey," he said. "I've lost my family and friends and I'm very tired and hungry."

The monkey smiled at Little Lion and put an arm around his shoulder. "Come and sit by me, Little Lion," he said. "I am your friend. You are safe now."

The wise old monkey gave him food and Little Lion ate until he was no longer hungry. Then he slept until he was no longer tired.

Later, the wise old monkey listened while Little Lion told him all that had happened. Then the monkey said, "Well done, Little Lion. Although all those animals said you were no good, you never gave up – you always kept on going. But it is true, you will never be King of the Jungle if you hide in a hole, or behind a rock, or in the reeds. Kings need castles," he said, "so you must have one."

Then the monkey began building the biggest and most brilliant sand castle that has ever been seen.

He put turrets round the walls and a special place for Little Lion to sit. At last, when he had finished, he stood back. "There is your castle," he said. "NOW you can be King of the Jungle."

Little Lion stepped into the castle. He felt so strong that he let out an enormous roar. Far away, his family and friends heard the roar and came running to find him.

Last to arrive was his father, who had been wounded by the hunters and could only walk slowly. He looked up at Little Lion, standing proudly in his castle, and said, "Little Lion, I see you are strong and brave. You have brought the family back together. You are now King of the Jungle."

And when Little Lion led his family back to their home, they passed the slithery snake, the horrid hyena and the cruel crocodile – who did not recognise him. They hid as he passed, not knowing that this King of the Jungle was the same little lion they had laughed at.

But he was.